WITHDRAWN

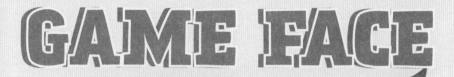

GAME FACE

Balancing Act

by Brigitte Cooper
illustrated by Tim Heitz

LOUIE LIN:
DANCING DYNAMO!

Calico

An Imprint of Magic Wagon
abdopublishing.com

For Louie: Your strength is an inspiration. For Geri & Clelia: Your support, my motivation. –BC

abdopublishing.com

THIS BOOK CONTAINS
RECYCLED MATERIALS

Written by Brigitte Cooper
Illustrated by Tim Heitz
Edited by Megan M. Gunderson
Art Directed by Laura Mitchell

Very special thanks to our content consultants, Scott Lauinger and Lana Clark!

Publisher's Cataloging-in-Publication Data

Names: Cooper, Brigitte, author. | Heitz, Tim, illustrator.
Title: Balancing act / by Brigitte Cooper; illustrated by Tim Heitz.
Description: Minneapolis, Minnesota : Magic Wagon, 2018. | Series: Game face
Summary: In order to work with a famous choreographer on her dance routine
for the state championship, Louie Lin reluctantly agrees to take Korean tea
ceremony lessons with her grandmother.
Identifiers: LCCN 2017946546 | ISBN 9781532130434 (lib.bdg.) | ISBN 9781532131035 (ebook) |
    ISBN 9781532131332 (Read-to-me ebook)
Subjects: LCSH: Dance--Juvenile fiction. | Self-reliance in adolescence--Juvenile fiction. |
    Korean tea ceremony--Juvenile fiction. | Grandparent and child--Juvenile fiction.
Classification: DDC [FIC]--dc23
LC record available at https://lccn.loc.gov/2017946546

TABLE OF CONTENTS

ONE

Dancing Dynamo

I was upside down. No, really. My feet soared through the air as my head whooshed over the springy foam mat.

A second earlier, I had completed the first of two consecutive back handsprings. In the blink of an eye, my body finished its rotation and my feet landed softly on the ground.

"Nice landing!" shouted Coach Amy.

I threw my arms in the air as I flashed a smile for the judges. Usually, I hated the showmanship that goes with competitions. How am I supposed to remember to smile when I'm tumbling all over? Today, however, every little point mattered.

It was the semifinal round of the Massachusetts Junior Rhythmic Gymnastics and Dance

Competition. Girls from all over the state were performing individual routines in hopes of making it to the state championships next month.

Technical, artistic, and execution judges watched our every move. They looked for the tiniest details that could separate the field. The smallest point deduction could make a difference.

So I showed off my smile again for the artistic judge.

"Keep it up, Louie!" shouted Coach Amy from the sidelines. "Focus until the finish."

I was in the middle of my routine. Things were going well. I had nailed my technical components. They included a front tuck, two balancing sequences, a series of back walkovers, and a pike jump. My limbs felt strong, the sign blood was pumping and sending energy from head to toe.

As I began my final sequence, the crowd clapped with the fast-paced music. I had picked a song that would hopefully get them involved in the performance. With only a few moves left, I was thankful for the energy their applause provided.

I danced from one end of the mat to the other, keeping my feet soft and my landings light. In rhythmic gymnastics and dance, choreography and tumbling mixed together into one powerful routine. That's why I loved the sport so much. Some athletes performed with a prop like a hoop, ribbon, or ball. In my division, dancers could perform freehand, with no equipment.

When I first started training with Coach Amy, I was five years old. I never could have imagined that I would be where I was today. Seconds away from finally clinching a spot in the state championships!

I finished my footwork and positioned myself in the corner of the mat, making sure not to step on the red out-of-bounds line. As the music picked up speed, I snuck a quick peek at the sidelines.

Coach Amy hovered nearby. The other girls from my dance team crowded around her. They had come to support me in the individual competition.

Behind them, my family sat in the front row of the stands. Dad's head darted back and forth, following my every move. Mom shielded her face, too nervous to watch. Halmeoni, my grandmother, sat perfectly still, her eyes on me.

I took a breath and visualized my final tumbling sequence. Two forward somersaults, followed by a no-handed cartwheel, and finish with a forward leap into a middle split.

In addition to showing perfect form, the key was to connect each element of the tumbling pass with little to no breaks. It was a difficult sequence. But I had practiced it hundreds of times over the past month for this very moment. I could do this.

"You got this, Louie!" shouted Rana.

Along with Maya and Alana, Rana sat a few rows above my parents. The girls were on their feet. They waved a sign that read Louie Lin: Dancing Dynamo! I chuckled, seeing it for the first time. It must have been Rana's idea.

Maya, Alana, Rana, and I had been friends since kindergarten. We did everything together. Even though none of them danced, they had never missed one of my competitions.

They smiled and enjoyed their own little dance party. It was the morale booster I needed to finish my routine with a bang.

I glanced at the clock. Ten seconds remained in my routine until time was up. If I went even a millisecond over, it would result in a point deduction.

I clenched my core, launching my body forward into the first of two somersaults. After

standing up, I lifted my hands into the air. Then I flung my body into a no-handed cartwheel, and tucked my chin to avoid throwing my head back.

My feet hit the ground firmly. I prepared for my forward leap, crouching down slightly to help build momentum. My hamstrings stretched and released as I jumped into the air, one leg in front of me, the other behind, toes pointed.

To finish it all off, I landed gracefully. Then I slid seamlessly into a split. I pulled my shoulders back and lifted my arms. I flashed one final smile for the judges.

The audience erupted in applause as the final note faded into the air.

"That's my girl!" shouted Dad.

Dad and Mom jumped to their feet.

"Well done, Louie!" added Mom, finally able to look.

As I jogged off of the mat, I noticed Rana, Alana, and Maya make their way down the stairs. They were headed straight for the scoring bench. That was the spot where I now had to await the final verdict.

"You nailed it!" shouted Coach Amy. She wrapped me in a bear hug as I exited the mat. "That was incredible! Not a single mistake. You must be so proud of yourself!"

"Thanks." I hugged her back. "But I don't want to celebrate just yet. Let's get the scores first."

Coach Amy tousled my short, black hair.

"Always a competitor," she laughed.

Coach Amy and I sat nervously on the bench. I chugged a bottle of water. Then I inspected the scoreboard hanging from the ceiling.

Elena was currently in first place. She had performed a flawless routine and was rewarded with a score of 18.0, very close to a perfect 20.0.

Suzanna was in second place. We had been on the same dance team for the past three years. She had bobbled slightly on one of her balancing skills. But she was close behind with a score of 17.5.

Lucy, in third place, was a dancer from Boston. She held on to a score of 16.5.

"Remember, the top three dancers advance to the state championships," whispered Coach Amy. "You only need to score higher than a 16.5 to make the cut."

I didn't need the reminder. We had built my entire routine knowing that I would need as many high scoring components as possible. It had been a risk, adding so many difficult moves.

I wondered if perhaps I should have been a bit more conservative in order to avoid deductions. I struggled to focus on the scoreboard.

"Does it always take this long for them to decide?" asked Alana.

The girls were now huddled above me on the closest bleacher bench.

"Sh," whispered Rana. "Don't stress me out. Look at Louie. Cool as a cucumber."

I laughed. Even in a room of a hundred people, I could still hear Rana's whisper.

Sweat dripped down my back and I shifted slightly in my seat. My heart rate was slowly making its descent back to normal. And I could feel my muscles aching to be stretched.

I glanced over to the judges table, their heads bent down, deep in conversation. I had to admit, it did seem to be taking them longer than usual.

"Is something wrong?" I asked Coach Amy.

She shrugged, eyes glued on the scoreboard.

Just when I couldn't take it any longer, the judges lifted their heads. They entered their decision into the keypad in front of them. My heart caught in my throat as flashing red numbers burst to life in front of my eyes.

"17.0!" shouted the announcer. "That does it, folks. Louie Lin wins third place and advances to the state championship!"

TWO

A Secret Plan

"These boxes go on forever!" said Maya as she looked around.

It was the following morning. Maya, Rana, and Alana were helping me tackle the attic during Lin Lane spring-cleaning day.

Lin Lane, our family store, was the only general store on the Cape. When my parents first moved to the sleepy seaside town from their home country of South Korea, they jumped at the opportunity to provide this much-needed business.

I was just a baby then, and Halmeoni hadn't come to live with us yet. My parents purchased a house in the center of town and turned the first floor into Lin Lane. Almost thirteen years later, it was one of the busiest stores in town.

We sold everything from neon tubes of sunscreen to colorful hooded sweatshirts, to cartons of organic milk and beyond. During the summer, the line snaked out the door and down the front steps as tourists waited patiently for freshly brewed coffee and a toasted bagel.

Last summer, Dad added six blue rocking chairs to the front porch. It quickly became a popular spot. Teenagers sat and enjoyed runny egg sandwiches. And children licked tasty treats from the nearby ice cream shop, the Scoop.

Lin Lane was one of the few stores to stay open year-round. That was one of the reasons business was booming. With the closest grocery store almost thirty minutes away, the locals took every opportunity to visit us for last minute must-haves during the blustery winter months.

"Honestly," said Rana, wrinkling her nose. "This room looks like it hasn't seen the light of day in years!"

She blew a layer of dust off of a nearby trunk and plopped down, taking a seat on the top. The tattered trunk looked familiar. But I couldn't quite remember what was inside.

Every year, toward the middle of spring, my parents enlisted our help for spring-cleaning day. With the busy season fast approaching, it was the perfect time to give the entire house a good scrubbing, top to bottom.

Everyone pitched in until the gray shingles sparkled like silver in the sunshine. We cleared cobwebs, wiped windows, and stocked shelves. This year, I was put on attic duty. I hated attic duty.

"Do you think we'll get a break soon?" asked Alana. "I'm starving. Didn't I see your grandmother in the kitchen earlier? Maybe she's making us something for lunch."

I glanced around, ready to take a break myself. My parents used the basement for inventory. We didn't have much space leftover for our own belongings. So, the attic was full of stuff we didn't want to get rid of, but had nowhere else to put.

We had been at it for almost two hours. We had organized bulky boxes, swept sandy corners, and folded piles of faded fabric. And still the room was a mess! Thankfully, the salty breeze from the open window had freshened up the musty air leftover from the room's hibernation.

"Let's just finish." I sighed. "I don't want to come back here when it's dark."

I stretched my arms overhead, eager for my afternoon practice with Coach Amy. We only had one month to choreograph, practice, and perfect my routine for the most important competition of my life. Every training session mattered.

"So," said Maya, reading my mind. "Are you excited for the state championship? I talked to Mac last night and he said I could cover it!"

Maya was the youngest and only female sports broadcaster in town. She covered every season of Cape Elementary School and Cape High School sports for our newspaper, the *Cape Chronicle*. Mac, her editor, was impressed with her work. He added other assignments like live broadcasting and high profile state competitions.

"That's awesome!" I said, giving her a fist pump.

"Yeah," she said. "Did you know that you and Suzanna are the first girls from the Cape to make it to the final round? I heard there are almost fifty dancers competing this year. The most ever!"

"Way to keep the pressure low," joked Alana. She dusted a pile of picture frames.

"That's nothing," added Rana. "Remember when she covered the Dodgers last softball season during playoffs? I thought I was going to have a nervous breakdown!"

Maya rolled her eyes.

"You didn't seem to mind when I wrote an entire article about your superior catching skills behind the plate," Maya said.

"What can I say? When you're right, you're right." Rana winked.

I laughed and lifted a heavy cardboard box of cookbooks onto a nearby shelf.

"Man, you are really strong," admired Alana. "I couldn't push that box across the floor if I wanted to. Maybe I'll do some weight lifting before ice hockey season this winter."

Alana was the smallest girl in our eighth grade class. She hadn't grown more than an inch since fifth grade. But she sure could eat like someone twice her size. Her tiny frame was an asset in the rink though. She could easily outskate the largest frozen foe.

"Nah, who am I kidding?" she continued, abandoning that idea. "I'd much rather spend my time in the Makerspace. That reminds me. My science journal only has a few empty pages left. I really should get a new one before next week's class."

I wiped the sweat from my brow and turned toward a teetering tower of tablecloths.

"Seriously," continued Maya. "What is your game plan, Louie? Off the record, of course."

"Well, I do have an idea," I said. I thought of the piece of paper I had tucked in my pocket. "Although I'm not sure my parents will go for it."

Rana's ears perked up instantly.

"A secret plan?" she asked. "Do tell!"

I hesitated, unsure whether or not to spill the beans. Based on the hungry look on Rana's face, I knew the cat was already out of the bag. I pulled the flyer from my pocket and handed it to her.

"I want to hire a choreographer," I explained. "And this one is the best."

Alana and Maya huddled around Rana. A glossy photo of an elegant woman stared back at them. Her long, brown hair was swept up in a colorful silk scarf. Shimmering gold earrings matched her glittery nail polish.

"Chloe Dupuis?" asked Maya. "Doesn't she have a studio in Boston?"

I nodded, not surprised that Maya had heard of her. Chloe Dupuis was a legend in the dance world.

A former prima ballerina from Paris, Chloe had transitioned into the world of rhythmic gymnastics and dance as a coach. She had worked with countless champions over her thirty-year career. As luck would have it, she had moved to the United States a few years ago.

"What about Coach Amy?" asked Rana. "You're not going to ditch her, are you?"

I shook my head.

"No way!" I said. "Coach Amy is the reason why I made it this far. I just feel like, in order to win the state championship, I need as much help as I can get. Especially with the artsy stuff."

"Are you allowed to hire a choreographer?" asked Alana.

"Yep," I answered. "It's not that uncommon for dancers to bring on an extra coach for big competitions. Coach Amy and I have talked about it and she would be on board."

"So, what's the hold up?" asked Rana, handing the paper back to me.

"My parents." I sighed. "I'm not sure they would allow it. I mentioned it last week to feel them out, but they didn't take the bait. It's kind of expensive. And they already spend a lot on my lessons with Coach Amy. I don't want to sound greedy, but I really think it could help."

Just then, something rustled from the far side of the room. I turned around to find Mom staring back at me.

"What is this I hear?" she asked.

She marched over and took the flyer from my hands, quickly scanning the words on the page. Silence hung heavy in the room as we waited for Mom's reaction.

"So, you want to hire a choreographer?" she asked.

I blushed. Even though I hadn't technically done anything wrong, I still felt guilty for talking about it behind her back.

"Well," I started, "she is considered one of the best. Coach Amy wouldn't mind, so it's not like we would hurt her feelings. It would only be for one month."

Mom hesitated, reading the words a second time.

"I understand if you don't want to," I quickly added. "It's OK, really. I shouldn't have brought it up."

Much to my surprise, Mom handed the paper back to me and smiled.

"I think it's a great idea," Mom said and patted me on the back. "This is the state championship, after all!"

My jaw practically hit the floor.

"Really?" I asked, dumbfounded.

"Really," she answered.

"Thank you!" I said, nearly knocking her down with a hug. "Thank you so much! I'll do extra chores and use my allowance to help pay for some of it. I promise!"

Mom laughed. Her dark brown eyes twinkled in the shadowy attic light.

"Oh, don't worry," she said. "I'm sure we will think of some way for you to earn it."

"You rock, Mrs. Lin!" said Rana, jumping off of the trunk.

A fragile clinking sound filled the air. Mom pointed to the trunk near her feet.

"Please be careful," she said. "That trunk holds my mother's most delicate belongings from South Korea, including her jade tea set. We're saving it for Louie. Maybe one day she'll be interested."

I realized now why the trunk looked familiar.

Each year, Mom and Halmeoni asked if I wanted to learn how to perform the traditional Korean tea ceremony for the Spring Blossom Festival. Each year, I said no. I had more interesting things to do than pour hot water from a rusty, old teapot.

Mom's eyes narrowed. I could tell an idea was forming in her mind. "You know what?" She glanced at the trunk. "I just thought of the perfect way for you to earn that choreography coach!"

THREE

Training

"Tea party lessons?" howled Coach Amy. "That's priceless!"

I rolled my eyes as I unpacked my equipment bag. Coach Amy had been pumped when I told her my parents said we could call Chloe Dupuis. Annoyingly, she had been even more enthusiastic about hearing the conditions of the deal.

Every morning before school, Halmeoni would give me Korean tea ceremony lessons. In three weeks, I would perform the ceremony at the Spring Blossom Festival. It was a yearly celebration hosted by the Cape Cultural Committee.

The committee organized events throughout the year for anyone interested in learning about different cultures and traditions. The Spring

Blossom Festival was my family's favorite, as it was dedicated solely to Korean culture. It was held in Town Park. And it included a day-long schedule of activities such as cooking demonstrations, musical performances, origami, arts and crafts, and, of course, the tea ceremony.

"I mean, you?" she said. "I can't wait to see it."

"OK, OK." I slipped off my leg warmers. "I get it. It's hilarious. Me, the tomboy, taking tea lessons. By the way, it's not a tea party. It's a tea ceremony. Besides, it's what I need to do in order to hire Chloe Dupuis. Can we move on now, please?"

I ripped a piece of lime green pre-wrap from its roll and fashioned it into a headband, pulling my bangs off of my face. Coach Amy wiped away tears and attempted to regain a straight face.

"Sure," she said. "Sorry. Let's stretch."

The Gym was a former warehouse on the edge of town. It was the only training facility for the Cape's gymnastics and dance teams.

The large, first floor room was used mostly for gymnastics equipment like the vault, balance beam, and uneven bars. Dance studios were upstairs, with shiny floors, mirrored walls, and a wooden ballet barre in each cavernous room.

My dance team inhabited both worlds. We used the various spaces to practice the different elements of our mixed routines.

Several teams could be practicing at once. The noisy chaos actually helped us prepare for competitions. It trained us to focus on our routines rather than getting distracted by others.

The Gym was fairly busy today. A team of peewee gymnasts worked at the balance beams. Their coaches hovered cautiously below them. The sound of synchronized tap dancing floated from the second floor as a few older girls swung powerfully from the uneven bars in the corner.

Coach Amy and I headed over to the large, springy floor mats. The floor was a resource for both gymnastics and dance. I spent most of my time there. I trained with the group dance team or worked privately with Coach Amy for individual rhythmic gymnastics competitions.

"Looks like Suzanna isn't wasting any time," I said, sinking into a hamstring stretch.

I nodded toward the other mat where Suzanna worked with Coach Mike, another coach from our dance team. She smiled and waved before launching into an impressive tumbling pass.

"Yeah," said Coach Amy. "Remember, even though you're competing against each other, you are still teammates at the end of the day."

Her constantly positive attitude was one of the reasons why I loved Coach Amy. When I got frustrated, she made me laugh. When my mood turned grumpy, she cracked a joke. When I wanted to give up, she made me continue.

A former Olympic gymnast, Coach Amy had moved back to the Cape to coach full-time. Her all-girls mentoring program, Strong Sisters, was popular around town. She also ran team building workshops at the elementary and high schools.

"So," I said, pushing up into a bridge, "when should we call her?"

"Already did," answered Coach Amy. "I spoke to her two months ago before someone else could snatch her up. I e-mailed her some videos of your recent competitions and she was very impressed. She'll be here at the end of the week."

I lowered my body, sat up, and stared in shock.

"What?" I asked, dumbfounded. "But we hadn't even finished semifinal rounds at that point. What if I didn't make it? Or my parents? What if they had said no?"

Coach Amy laughed and swatted at my toes.

"I knew you would make it," she said. "And, let's just say your parents have known for a while."

"Unbelievable," I said in disbelief. "Were the tea ceremony lessons part of the plan all along, too?"

Coach Amy stood and stretched her arms overhead.

"Nope," she said. "That was an unexpected surprise! Now, let's warm up."

I jumped to my feet, energized by the good news. I ran ten laps around the mat, alternating between jogging and sprinting, followed by high knees and handstand walks. After a three minute plank, twenty push-ups, and fifty lunges, my muscles were ready to go.

"So, Louie," said Coach Amy, handing me my wrist guards. "Have you thought about what you want the theme to be?"

A strong routine needed to have a clear theme. While tumbling was my favorite part, there were other things we needed to pay attention to. Good flow, artistic elements, and music choice were also important to the judges.

Over the years, we had chosen fun and creative themes. Last year, for regional competitions, we used the theme of water. I wore a blue leotard and moved fluidly in and out of somersaults to the soft, wave-like tunes of a cello concerto.

Another fun theme had been the Wild West where I sprinted around the floor to a fast-paced guitar riff. I finished with a series of back walkovers meant to represent a bucking bronco ride.

But there was one theme in particular that I had been saving until now. "Yes," I said. "I know exactly what I want the theme to be. Strength."

"Strength?" repeated Coach Amy.

"Think about it," I answered. "What's the one thing that all rhythmic dancers need? Strength. It covers all aspects of our sport. Endurance, commitment, agility. What better way to show the judges I should win than to be the strongest performer on the mat?"

Coach Amy bit her lip, thinking for a second.

"That could work, I suppose. You are going to need to show a variety of strong technical skills."

"Exactly." I nodded, happy that she liked my idea. "For music, I thought a loud rock song would catch the judge's attention and set me apart from the other girls."

I tightened the Velcro straps on my wrist guards, itching to get started.

"Let's work on some technical stuff first," said Coach Amy. "Then we can put together some options for tumbling passes. When Chloe arrives, we'll show her what we've got and see what she thinks. Remember, it needs to be artistic, too."

"Sounds like a plan," I said, confident I could also convince Chloe of my plan.

We high-fived and headed toward the corner of the mat. I spent the rest of practice putting together a variety of difficult tumbling passes. We wanted to consider all of our options and decide which skills were strongest.

In rhythmic gymnastics and dance, it was important to avoid movements that landed abruptly in a vertical position. Instead, skills needed to flow seamlessly into the next move, giving the routine the fluid feel of a dance.

We worked on every combination we could think of in order to determine what flowed best together.

"I liked that last pass," Coach Amy said after awhile. "Let's try that again, then take a quick water break."

I jogged back to the corner, tucked my hips, and squared my shoulders. Then I sprinted forward. After a few steps, I swung my arms down to the ground to begin the first of two cartwheels.

My legs lifted off the mat as I used my upper body strength to push me the rest of the way. When I landed the second cartwheel, I let my front leg slide forward, bringing my entire body down into a split.

Flexibility was something the judges looked for. I made sure to stretch my legs the full 180 degrees.

I then lowered my forearms to the mat and used my core muscles to draw my legs up into the air, moving into a difficult elbow stand. Next, I tucked my chin and let my body fall forward into a somersault, then up to standing.

I separated my feet slightly, lifted up through my rib cage, and rose onto relevé, or tiptoe. Maintaining perfect balance, I twirled twice, completing a circle before lowering onto flat feet.

"Excellent!" said Coach Amy. "We definitely should use that sequence somehow."

I sprinted off the mat and grabbed my water bottle. The refreshing liquid hit the spot after almost an hour of intense tumbling. From the corner of my eye, I noticed Suzanna working on an equally impressive sequence of her own.

Coach Amy reached into my equipment bag and pulled out two ankle weights.

"Let's finish with legs today," Coach Amy said. She tossed me the sand-filled straps.

I had never used ankle weights until Coach Amy suggested it a few years ago. The idea was, if I could jump high and stretch my legs long while wearing the heavy weights, I would jump higher and stretch longer without them.

I quickly wrapped the weights around my ankles, and jogged back to the center of the mat. I spent the final twenty minutes of practice working on forward leaps, tucks, and pike jumps.

"Great work," said Coach Amy at the end of practice. "Now, get some rest. We're back at it tomorrow."

As I pedaled home in the pale evening light, a seagull squawked overhead. It kept pace with my bike, challenging me to a race along the dunes.

"You're on!" I whispered, pumping my legs and gaining speed. I was determined to reach the imaginary finish line first.

FOUR

Tea Party Lessons

The smell of greasy cheese wafted teasingly across the table.

"Do you think we should order another pizza?" asked Alana. She refilled her plastic cup with a frothy stream of lemon lime soda.

It was a few days later. After my training session, I ran to meet the girls for dinner. We decided on Pete's, the Cape's best pizza parlor. We were sitting at our favorite red and white checkered booth in the back.

"Might as well," said Rana. She grabbed a napkin to wipe a dribble of grease from her chin. "In a few weeks, this place will be packed. We might not even be able to get a table, let alone a second pie."

Alana nodded and motioned for the waitress. She quickly brought over a piping hot replacement for our empty tray.

"Aren't you going to have another slice?" Alana asked me.

I swallowed the last bit of buttery crust and stared longingly at my empty plate.

"Nah," I said, wiping my mouth with a napkin. "One slice is my limit during training. As soon as the championship is over, though, we're coming back here. And then I'm getting a whole pizza just for me."

Alana shrugged and reached for her third slice.

"Your loss," she said, popping the cheesy bubbles with her fingers.

Maya reached for the pencil tucked into her curly ponytail and scribbled some notes in her journal.

"Do you think Chloe Dupuis would sit down for an interview with me?" she asked. "I'd love to get some quotes from her about what the judges might be looking for. When do you start working with her again?"

I pushed the tempting tray far across the table. "Tomorrow afternoon," I said. "I can't wait."

"When do your tea lessons start?" asked Rana.

"Ugh," I said, remembering the other end of the bargain. "Tomorrow morning."

"I bet your grandmother is excited," Rana said. She shook a large dose of garlic salt onto her pizza.

"Yeah," I admitted. "She had me carry that heavy trunk down from the attic last night. She wanted to polish her tea set for our lessons. Still, waking up at the crack of dawn to pour tea? There's nothing I'd rather do less."

Rana laughed.

"It might not be as bad as you think," she said. "A few years ago, my grandmother spent the whole summer with us. She wanted to teach me how to cook her favorite Persian food. At first, it was a pain because it was softball season. And I really needed to work on extra batting practice."

"So what did you do?" I asked, surprised to hear this new story.

Rana shrugged and polished off the final slice.

"I was busier than usual, but it all worked out. And it was actually pretty cool. By the end of the summer, I had spent quality time with my grandmother and could cook a bunch of new dishes. And I still played great behind the plate!"

We paid for our pizzas and walked to the parking lot. Billy, Alana's oldest brother, was waiting for us in the O'Brien family station wagon.

"Hey guys!" he said. His bright red hair and freckles matched Alana's. "Timmy's working the counter at the Scoop tonight. Anybody up for a Seagull Sundae?"

Timmy, another of the three O'Brien boys, always managed to sneak us extra toppings when we paid him a visit.

"It's an added perk, since I'm the only girl in the family," Alana liked to say.

As we made our way along the sleepy streets, the car tires crunched against scattered seashells.

"When is the Spring Blossom Festival?" asked Maya. She somehow managed to scribble from her squished spot in the middle seat. "Are you worried it will interfere with the state championship?"

"No way," I said. "It's the weekend before. Let's move on, because I have a question for you. Who is going to give me a taste of their sundae?"

The following morning, my alarm beeped at 6:00 a.m. I groaned, smacked the menacing machine, and rolled over for another five minutes. Before I could reach the cool side of the pillow, my bedroom door opened.

"Up and at 'em, madam," whispered Halmeoni.

I smiled. I had heard her use that phrase a million times before. But it still sounded silly in her thick accent.

When my grandfather died five years ago, Halmeoni left South Korea and came to live with us. She had learned an impressive amount of English in that time. But quirky phrases and rhymes seemed to be her favorite.

"Put this on," she said, placing a folded fabric on my bed. "Then come to my room in five minutes."

With that, she shuffled her slippers across the hardwood floor and left. I rubbed the sleep from my eyes, took a few deep breaths, and pulled myself out of bed. I looked at the soft, pink fabric. It was a *hanbok*, a traditional Korean dress.

"Great," I muttered, touching the delicate silk. "Tea and dress up. Two of my favorite things."

As I walked down the narrow hallway toward Halmeoni's room, I could hear my parents opening up the shop below. The bitter smell of coffee wafted up from the kitchen, jarring my sleepy senses.

I knocked softly on Halmeoni's door and entered quietly. The soft strums of the *gayageum*, a Korean guitar, played from the stereo on her bedside table.

"You look beautiful," said Halmeoni from her spot in the center of the floor. Her small frame rested on folded knees.

She was wearing a sky blue *hanbok* that tied across the chest in a bright raspberry bow. Unlike mine, which was all one color, her dress had a petal pink skirt and crisp, white cuffs at the neck and wrists. Her silky black hair was pulled into a low bun, showing off her long, elegant neck and deep, dark eyes.

"So do you," I said, awed for a moment by my grandmother's beauty. "I've never seen you wear that *hanbok* before. Is it new?"

Halmeoni smiled and gestured for me to sit next to her.

"It belonged to my grandmother," she said. "And one day it will belong to you. I have been saving it for a special occasion. I have waited a long time to teach you about our culture's most respected tradition. That day is finally here. Why not dress accordingly?"

I blushed, feeling guilty for my bad attitude, and took a seat. Halmeoni removed a red linen napkin from the wooden tray in front of her.

On the tray sat a ceramic tea set made of deep green jade. The set included a lidded teapot, two round containers, a wooden spoon, and a large bowl. Three small cups sat in a row on the right side of the tray. A black, cast-iron tea kettle rested on a hot plate. Steam swirled from its spout.

"As you already know, the Korean word for this tea ceremony is *darye*, which translates roughly to 'tea etiquette,' " Halmeoni explained. "The beauty of *darye* is its simplicity. It is a deliberate and elegant process that allows one to stop, relax, and enjoy."

I nodded. My eager muscles already started to twitch beneath me.

"First, we must pay attention to how we sit during *darye*," Halmeoni said softly. "Even though we are on the floor, we cannot be lazy. Keep your back straight, your shoulders strong, and chin up."

She gently nudged me in the ribs, forcing me to sit a bit taller.

"Good," she said. "Now let's begin."

Halmeoni reached for the bamboo handle of the tea kettle. Then she poured a stream of hot liquid into the large, ceramic bowl. After a few minutes, she removed the lid from the teapot and transferred the liquid from the bowl into the pot.

"Wait," I said, already confused. "Why don't you just pour the water from the kettle directly into the teapot?"

"Patience, my dear," she answered. "Green tea is best served at eighty degrees. The water from the kettle is still boiling hot. Pouring it into the bowl first allows it to cool."

I nodded, not convinced that the extra step was needed.

Next, Halmeoni poured another batch of water from the kettle into the ceramic bowl and set it off to the side. Then, she lifted the teapot and filled the three cups with the clear, cooled liquid.

"Wait," I said. "You forgot to add tea leaves."

Halmeoni continued to pour, her arms flowing gracefully over the cups. She moved carefully, making sure not to splash.

"We will not actually be drinking this," she explained. "This liquid prewarms the cups so that they are at the ideal temperature when the tea is ready. The farthest cup is for our most respected guest. The host's is closest to him or her. Start with your guests, and work backwards, so that their cups will be warm for the longest amount of time."

When she finished filling each cup, she set the teapot back on the tray.

"But now the pot is empty," I said. "How do we make tea?"

Halmeoni picked up the bowl. And, for a second time, poured its cooled water into the pot. Then, she removed the lid from one of the small containers on the tray, revealing a pile of dark green leaves.

She placed her delicate hands on her lap, closed her eyes, and took a few soft breaths.

"Now," she whispered, "we make the tea."

I clenched my jaw, trying to mask my rising frustration. I glanced quickly at the clock. Fifteen minutes had passed and still there was no sign of tea. At this rate, I'd be lucky to get a sip before the state championship started.

FIVE

Chloe Dupuis

"She's late," I said for the fifth time in thirty minutes.

Coach Amy and I sat in the ballet studio, anxiously awaiting Chloe Dupuis' arrival. The school day hadn't gone much faster than my morning *darye* lesson. The excitement of meeting the famous choreographer was too much to bear.

"She's not late, Louie. She's just not early."

I walked over to the wooden barre that ran the length of the mirrored wall. I had already warmed up, but could feel my muscles starting to get cold. I lifted my right leg and placed it on the bar, stretching my upper body across it.

Suddenly, a noise came from the corner of the room.

"Point your toes," said a voice. "And, for heaven's sake, unclench your fists!"

I lifted my head and looked into the mirror. There, staring back at me, was Chloe Dupuis.

Her long, lean body was covered in black spandex. Her ballet slippers were pastel pink. Her chestnut brown hair was parted at the side and pulled into a low bun. A silk floral scarf, similar to the one from her photo, was tied around her neck.

She did not wear a stitch of makeup, but her cheeks were naturally rosy, her eyelashes thick and full. On her fingernails, she wore her signature glittery gold polish.

"Bonjour," she said in a heavy French accent. "I am Mademoiselle Chloe Dupuis. You must be Olivia, no?"

I hadn't been called by my full name in ages. The word sounded foreign to my ears.

"Please, call me Louie," I said as politely as possible.

Before I had a chance to lower myself from the barre, Chloe dropped her bag and stood next to me. She pressed her delicate fingers into the fleshy underside of my foot, pushing my toes into a more pointed position.

Next, she took my hands. She stretched them open, pulling my fingers as far as they could go.

"There, you see?" she said. She stood back to admire her work. "Much better."

I released the barre. I turned to her, angry at myself for not making a stronger first impression.

"Yes," I said, shaking her hand. "Thank you."

"It's a pleasure to meet you, Mademoiselle Dupuis," said Coach Amy.

"Please, call me Chloe," she said. "We are all friends now. I was very impressed with your videos, Louie," she continued. "I think you have quite the shot at winning the, how do you say? Whole shebang?"

She chuckled at her own joke and I relaxed slightly.

"Thank you," I said. "I'm very excited to work with you. Especially on the artistic elements of my routine."

The hint of a frown flashed across Chloe's face.

"Ah, yes," she said. "That is what I want to start with. Do you know why I adjusted you just now?"

"Because it was not proper form," I answered matter-of-factly.

"Not exactly," Chloe answered. "True, your form was off. But, more importantly, a dancer must be graceful at all times. Even while stretching. In order to dance beautifully, one must live beautifully. Art imitates life, does it not?"

Chloe lifted her arms overhead, leaned forward slightly, and raised her back leg behind her. She remained perfectly still in an arabesque position.

"For example," she explained, "take the arabesque position. It is really no different than if I were running down the street after the beret that had just been blown off my head by the wind."

She jumped slightly and reached her fingers, grasping for the imaginary hat. She landed softly, her pink slippers barely making a sound on the polished floor. She finished with a curtsy.

"You see?" she asked. "I hope you don't mind, but I looked at your competition scores from the past year. You are a strong athlete. But even the strongest competitors have a weakness. Do you know what yours is, Louie?"

I shifted uncomfortably, not sure I liked where this conversation was headed.

"Artistic score," she answered. "So, in order to help you grow as a performer, I think we must build the most wonderfully artistic routine of your life. Elegant footwork. Soft music. Of course, we'll incorporate the required tumbling skills, but our main theme will be the beauty of the dance. That should get the judges attention, no?"

She smiled, awaiting my response. I looked nervously at Coach Amy.

"Well," I started, "it's just we sort of thought the theme for my routine could be strength. You know? Powerful moves. Fast pace. Loud music."

Chloe stared back, considering my idea. When she said nothing, I charged ahead.

"I've been working on some pretty difficult tumbling passes that the judges should like," I said. "Why don't we go downstairs to the floor mats and I can show you?"

Chloe shook her head.

"Perhaps next time," she said, untying the silk scarf from her neck. "Today, we should stay in the studio so that I can assess your artistic strengths."

I hesitated, surprised at how this was going. Sensing my frustration, Coach Amy came to my side and nudged me forward.

"Great idea," she said. "Right Louie?"

"Sure," I grunted, trying to keep my voice calm.

I unzipped my bag and pulled out a pair of black ballet shoes. I slipped them on, instantly constricted by the tight elastic strap. Normally, I practiced barefoot, but something told me Chloe would not approve of that.

As I stood up, something poked the underside of my right foot. I took a closer look, mortified to find the tag of the slipper still attached to the sole. I ripped it off, hoping Chloe hadn't noticed, and shoved it quickly back into my bag.

"Let's begin with the classical ballet positions," Chloe began. "Can you show me first position?"

I couldn't remember the last time I practiced positions. Thankfully, it was a lot like riding a bike. The moves weren't difficult to remember.

I pressed my heels together and let my feet open into a natural turned out position. With thighs touching, I stood tall, using my core strength to keep me balanced. Then, I rounded my arms in front of my chest as if holding a giant beach ball.

"Very good," Chloe said, circling my body. "Now, second position please."

With my feet still turned out, I stepped my legs apart, creating a small gap between them. I opened my arms out to the sides, as well, keeping them rounded and lifted.

"Chin up," Chloe said. She tapped the underside of my chin with her finger. "Third, please."

I closed the gap between my legs, stepping my right foot directly in front of my left, heel in front of toe. I kept my feet flat, my knees soft. With my right arm out to the side, I brought the left in front of my belly button.

"Beautiful," Chloe said, still circling. "And fourth?"

I stepped my right foot forward, keeping my toes turned out. Next, I changed arm positions. I brought my left hand in front of my belly button and the right above my head. I stretched my fingers as far as they could go, determined not to make the same mistake twice.

"Chest open," she said, pulling my shoulders back. "Now, on to fifth."

To finish, I lifted my left arm to meet the right and ended with a plié. Then, I waited for a reaction. Chloe circled me a few more times, silently assessing my form.

I glanced at Coach Amy, wondering what was going through her head. Finally, Chloe clapped.

"*Oui*," she said. "Just as I suspected. You have tremendous artistic potential. We just need to develop it further. No time to waste!"

She reached into her bag and pulled out a giant roll of duct tape. She ripped off a strip with her dazzlingly white teeth.

I watched curiously. She taped out a large box with an X in the middle, the lines bright against the sandy hardwood. When she finished, she placed the tape back in her bag and pointed at the strange design.

"Now," she explained, "step inside the box. And let's do that again."

I sighed and thought of the empty floor mat waiting for me on the first floor. The odds of seeing it quickly slipped away.

SIX

Sleepover

"What are you doing, Louie?" asked Rana.

The following Friday, the girls came over for a sleepover. It had been an unusually mild day, so we set up camp on the porch.

The soft breeze from the nearby ocean pushed the rocking chairs back and forth. The glowing afternoon sun cast a golden shadow across the lawn, encouraging newly budding flowers to emerge from their winter sleep.

Maya and Alana were working on a crossword puzzle. Rana wove friendship bracelets out of colorful yarn. A large bowl of uncooked rice rested on my lap, my right hand plunged deep inside.

"It's to help build wrist strength," I explained. "I'm tracing every letter of the alphabet on the

bottom of the bowl. The rice makes it harder for my wrist to move."

I finished the letter Z and swapped hands. I pushed my left fist into the smooth grains.

"I need to make sure I don't lose muscle strength. Especially since I'm not tumbling as much these days," I said.

A cascade of rice fell over the side after an aggressive *E*.

"Whoa, take it easy," said Alana. She scooped up the fallen rice. "No need to waste good food."

She dropped the handful into the bowl. Then she plucked a cookie from the tin on the front step.

"Maya, do you think your sister would give me the recipe for these snickerdoodles? They're delicious!" she said. "Or maybe I can try to figure it out on my own. That could be a fun experiment. Baking is a science, after all!"

I looked longingly at the pile of golden brown treats.

"Oh, what the heck," I said. I set the bowl on the floor. "Pass me one of those."

Alana tossed me a cookie and I swallowed it in one bite. The warm nutmeg and spicy cinnamon danced on my deprived taste buds.

"How's training going?" asked Maya.

I wiped a trail of crumbs from my lips.

"So-so," I said. "I don't feel like my routine is coming together just yet. I've been nailing my tumbling passes with Coach Amy. But the choreography is still an issue. So far, Chloe has spent all of our practices in the studio."

I resumed my wrist work, keeping my hands busy to avoid having a second cookie.

"But I thought you liked to dance?" asked Maya, confused.

"I do." I sighed. "But not this fancy stuff we're doing. If I have to plié one more time, I'm going to lose it! The problem is, in order to get enough power to complete the difficult tumbling passes, I need to build up speed. Normally, I sprint across the mat to gain momentum . . ."

"Let me guess," interrupted Alana. "Chloe prefers delicate footwork, which doesn't give you the necessary power. Am I right?"

"Yes!" I answered. "Exactly. How did you know?"

"It's basic physics," Alana continued. "An object in motion stays in motion. It's the same on the hockey rink. Even though I'm tiny, I build power by moving my skates across the ice. Once momentum kicks in, I'm a force to be reckoned with!"

"Yeah, well, all of this studio work is cutting into valuable tumbling time on the mat," I said. "I thought maybe I could add morning practices to the schedule. But my lessons with Halmeoni get in the way of that."

"How are those going?" asked Rana.

She snipped a thread and finished her bracelet with a double knot. She inspected her craftsmanship before beginning another.

I thought of this morning's *darye* lesson. Halmeoni had spent fifteen minutes reviewing the proper way to scoop the tea leaves from their container.

"Ugh," I grunted. "Don't ask."

Just then, the screen door swung open.

Mom stepped onto the porch. She had a large cardboard box in her hands.

"Girls," she said. "Can you please help me fold these beach towels? I want the shelves to be fully stocked for Spring Fling tomorrow."

Rana smiled and took the box.

"Sure thing!" she said, dropping the box at my feet. "Folding is also good for wrist strength, right?"

"Indeed!" Mom winked before returning inside.

I abandoned the rice and opened the stiff, cardboard flaps, revealing an assortment of terry cloth towels. The fabric was soft and pillowy, a welcome relief for my tired hands.

"What's our strategy for tomorrow?" asked Rana, reaching into the box.

On the Cape, only a handful of places like Lin Lane stayed open all year round. Most of the other stores took a break once summer tourists returned home and the streets cleared out.

Every year, on Spring Fling, the shops reopened. They welcomed the oncoming season with sidewalk parties, tasty treats, and live music. Everyone in town participated. Coach Amy even canceled our session so we could enjoy the festivities.

"I want to go to the Paper Store," said Maya. "I've been dreaming about their pen aisle all winter long."

"The pen aisle?" Rana laughed. "I love you, Maya, but you're such a word nerd!"

Alana plopped down and tipped the cardboard box on its side.

"I need to stop by Harry's Hardware," she said, "to get some replacement tools for my STEAM kit. I can't find my tape measure anywhere."

Rana nodded, making mental note of our itinerary.

"Let's also go to the Mermaid's Chair," she said. "I heard Mrs. Arielle is hosting a fashion show to highlight the new summer collection. What about you, Louie? What's on your agenda?"

I shrugged my shoulders and sighed.

"Oh, come on," said Rana, nudging me in the ribs. "You, of all people, hate a pity party. This is Spring Fling we're talking about! I heard the Clam Strip is going to give away free lobster rolls. How can you be gloomy at a time like this?"

I smiled. Even in my grumpiest moods, Rana knew just what to say.

"Well," I admitted, "I've been looking forward to checking out the new comic book selection at the Book Nook."

Rana slapped her knee and laughed.

"See?" she said. "You're happier already. Trust me. All you need is a fun day off to clear your head. Next week's training will be better. I just know it."

Rana handed me another towel. We continued folding as the sinking sun fell further in the spring sky.

The following morning, I awoke to the smell of cotton candy wafting through my open bedroom window. At some point in the night, I must have abandoned the group, leaving my sleeping bag in favor of my comfy quilt.

"Hey, what gives?" asked Maya, rolling over in her tangled mess of blankets. "I didn't know the bed was an option!"

Rana and Alana burrowed out of their bags.

"Yum," said Alana, sniffing the air. "I want to eat that smell!"

I pushed the window open farther, a sugary sweet breeze filling the room.

"Happy Spring Fling!" I shouted. "Let's get this party started!"

SEVEN

Respect

By ten thirty in the morning, Lin Lane was completely packed.

"This place is a madhouse!" said Rana.

We were standing near the front steps of the store, handing out complimentary bottles of sunscreen. Halmeoni circled the crowd, offering green tea in paper cups.

"Thank you, girls," said Dad when we returned the empty trays to the cash register. "Now, off you go. Enjoy the afternoon!"

After a brisk bike ride, we made our way to Main Street, pushing through the crowd. Balloons bopped down the streets, their white strings tied snuggly around toddlers' wrists. A jazz trio's tunes filled the air, the songs lively and whimsical.

"Jackpot!" said Alana. She pointed to the nearby Candy Bazaar.

Porky, the owner, stood outside wearing a clown outfit. A cotton candy machine hummed as people waited for their treat.

We spent the next hour at the Book Nook, where
I splurged on two new installments of my favorite
comic series. We also stopped by the Paper Store,
where Maya bought every color gel pen.

Soon, my stomach started to rumble and my thoughts turned to lunch.

"Let's investigate that lobster roll situation," I suggested.

"OK," agreed Rana. "But don't think you're getting out of going to the Mermaid's Chair."

I rolled my eyes. A fashion show was the last thing on my mind. By the time we arrived at Lambert's Beach, there was only one picnic table left.

Maya offered to save our seats as the rest of us stood in line nearby at the Clam Strip, the Cape's famous spot for seafood. A line of families eager for the first taste of the season extended deep into the gravel parking lot.

Lambert's Beach was one of my favorite areas on the Cape. It offered something special in every part of the year.

During the busy summer months, the waves provided endless hours of boogie boarding fun. In the fall, the warm sand was the perfect spot for a picnic. When winter hit, the dunes turned into sledding hills. On a spring day like today, the sea washed up a variety of interesting artifacts onto the shore.

"Hey, look," said Alana, pointing toward the front of the line. "There's Lara and Dottie. Maybe they want to sit with us, too."

I craned my neck and noticed a group of kids from our class at the takeout window. Their trays were piled high with grease-soaked cartons of food.

Lara and Dottie were two of the oldest, and coolest, girls in our grade. They played on the Dodgers with us during summer softball. Dottie was nice on and off the field. Lara sometimes gave Rana a hard time for her low batting average.

"Fine," said Rana, clearly not psyched about the idea. "But if Lara starts giving me tips about proper bunting form again, I'm out of here."

I grinned and gave her a playful poke.

"Aw come on," I said, the salty spring air relaxing my nerves. "You said it yourself. Free lobster rolls! How can you be gloomy at a time like this?"

As we enjoyed our food, I felt my tensions melt away. By the time we finished our root beer floats and a walk on the beach, I was feeling good. So good, in fact, that I didn't even put up a fight when Rana remembered the fashion show.

The following morning, I awoke energized and upbeat. I couldn't wait for my afternoon training session, confident that today would be the day we made some real progress. All that stood in the way was my morning *darye* lesson.

"You're moving too quickly, my love," said Halmeoni. She wiped up a splash of spilled liquid. "How can your guests enjoy their tea if it is splattered all over the place? Remember, there is beauty in stillness."

I tugged at the collar of my *hanbok*, the silk suddenly hot and tight around my neck. For the second time that morning, I had forgotten to hold the teapot lid firmly in place as I poured the tea.

"I'm sorry," I said. The liquid stained my skirt a deeper shade of pink. "I will try to be more careful."

Reluctantly, I started the detailed process all over again.

I warmed the teacups and allowed the water in the pot to cool. Then, I reached for the container of tea leaves. I shook the jar, remembering to gently roll the leaves onto the wooden spoon so as not to break them. Next, I carefully dropped the leaves into the water and waited for them to steep.

After a few moments of silence, Halmeoni nodded. "What's next?" she asked.

I hesitated, trying to remember the various steps. For something as simple as pouring tea, this process was surprisingly complicated.

"The host pours tea in his or her cup first," I explained. "To make sure it is ready before serving it to guests."

Halmeoni smiled.

"Very good," she answered.

I reached for the cup farthest from me, about to dump out the warming water. Halmeoni placed her hand on mine and shook her head.

"That cup belongs to the most honored guest," she said. She redirected me to the host's cup closest to me.

My cheeks grew warm and my neck started to itch. How was I supposed to remember all of these details? The guitar music in the background sounded like nails on a chalkboard. I took a deep breath and tried to remain calm.

"Yes. I remember now," I said through gritted teeth.

Once the cups were emptied, I poured a bit of tea into my own. The liquid was a translucent shade of celery green, the sign that it had finished steeping and was ready to be poured.

"Slowly this time," instructed Halmeoni.

Carefully, I began pouring the tea. I moved the teapot back and forth over the row, pouring only a little bit in each cup at a time. I could sense Halmeoni's eyes following my every move.

When all of the liquid had been distributed, I placed the teapot back on the tray. I waited as Halmeoni made her inspection.

"Excellent," she admired. "The liquid levels are even and the color is balanced. The taste should be lovely. Time to serve."

I glanced at the clock, wondering how much time was left. I wanted to stretch my muscles and get outside. Instead, I arranged three wooden coasters on the tray.

"Facedown," whispered Halmeoni.

I looked at her, confused.

"What?" I asked.

"The coasters," she said. "They have pictures on them. So you must place them facedown as a sign of respect."

I wondered how the colorful flowers on the coaster could somehow be seen as disrespectful. But I flipped them over anyway and moved on. Next, I placed each cup on a coaster. I remembered to keep one hand below the other, the proper form to prevent my sleeve from dipping into the liquid.

"As the host," Halmeoni said, "you take the first three sips as one last way to ensure the tea is ready. Do you remember what each sip is for?"

I took hold of my cup, one hand on the side, the other on the bottom. Proper hand placement was also a sign of respect.

The earthy aroma of the liquid reminded me of vegetables. In *darye*, green tea was served traditionally with no added sugars to sweeten it. Normally, I didn't mind the taste. But I had sipped enough tea over the past weeks to last a lifetime.

"The first is to enjoy the color," I began. "The second is to admire the aroma and the third is to savor the taste."

Halmeoni nodded quietly. Her coaster rested delicately on her lap. With her approval, I took three sips.

"As my most respected guest," I said after finishing, "please, enjoy."

Halmeoni smiled and lifted the cup to her lips. She closed her eyes and took three sips. I snuck a look at the clock, relieved to see only five minutes remained before I had to get ready for school.

"This is quite good, Louie," said Halmeoni. She placed her cup back on the tray. "Quite good, indeed. I have no doubt that you will do just fine at the Spring Blossom Festival."

I thought for a second that maybe, just maybe, she would say that we could stop our lessons. Then, I could spend my mornings at the Gym on some much needed extra training.

"However, the experience of *darye* is one to be enjoyed, not rushed," she said. "Perhaps I will add some research into our lessons, so that you can understand its importance in our culture. The guests at the festival are esteemed friends of our family. You must first respect the beauty of the ceremony in order to show them that you fully understand it."

Her words struck a nerve. They reminded me of Chloe. And the countless hours we had been devoting to pointing toes, stretching fingers, and lengthening limbs. I placed my cup down and gave Halmeoni a quick hug.

"Sorry," I said, leaving my tea unfinished. "Got to go!"

Then I rushed out of the room without taking a fourth sip.

EIGHT

Virtuosity

The springy bounce of the floor mat never felt so good beneath my toes. A week later, I arrived at the Gym earlier than usual. My final period history class with Mrs. Summerhill had been unexpectedly cancelled.

Thankfully, Coach Amy was free. We started practice early, giving us a few minutes alone before Chloe would arrive.

"I missed this," I said, sinking into a hip stretch.

"Oh, don't be so dramatic," laughed Coach Amy. "You make it sound like we haven't been on the mats in weeks."

I swiveled onto my stomach and pressed up into a cobra stretch. I breathed deeply to fill my lungs with air.

"Well, it sure feels that way to me," I said. "Maybe it's because we still haven't finalized my theme. Don't you think we should do that soon? The competition is two weeks away and we haven't even picked my song. I'm starting to freak out!"

"Yeah," she admitted. "We need to nail it down today."

Finding a theme that Chloe and I could agree on was proving to be nearly impossible. We were polar opposites. When I said fast, she said slow. When I said strong, she said soft. When I said powerful, she said elegant. Poor Coach Amy was stuck in the middle, trying to keep the peace.

"I still think strength is the best theme," I said, finishing my warm-up with a split.

"Trust me," she laughed. "You've made that clear. Now, let's work on that new tumbling pass."

I hopped up and strapped on my wrist guards. I had been working on this sequence all week and was excited to incorporate it into the routine.

It was the perfect combination of all of my strengths. Tumbling, flexibility, balance, and footwork. I positioned myself in the far corner of the mat. As I visualized the steps, I mentally checked off each move.

I forced out a puff of air and tightened my abdominal muscles. Core strength was key in tumbling. Without it, a dancer was doomed.

I rolled my shoulders, moving my neck back and forth. A series of cracks vibrated down my spine as I squeezed my shoulder blades together.

I clenched my fists to flex my biceps and triceps. I would need as much upper-body strength as possible to complete this difficult sequence. When I felt ready, I lifted my right knee and fell forward into a sprint.

The pass started with two regular cartwheels into an aerial, no-handed cartwheel. I landed all three no problem. Next, I began a combination of handstand pirouettes. With my legs up in the air, I swiveled and swirled my hands in small, intricate movements, twirling my body around in circles across the mat.

Then, I fell out of my handstand and into a bridge. Using my core strength, I kicked off the mat and brought my legs back into the air above my head. Moving into a mid-air split, I lowered each leg in opposite directions. Then I brought them together and launched into standing position.

"Beautiful!" cheered Coach Amy. "Keep it up!"

After another series of cartwheels, I moved into a balancing interlude.

I rose on to relevé, my entire body propped up by the tiptoe of my right foot. I swooped my arms upward, using the momentum to twist my body around in two rotations. The trickiest part of this sequence involved my left leg, which I pulled up flush against my body, chin grazing shin.

"Here we go!" shouted Coach Amy. "Strong finish!"

Next, I completed a series of three quick leaps. I led with my right leg, then left leg, and finished with a lateral leap, tapping my toes mid-air to show added flexibility.

Finally, I positioned myself in the opposite corner. I sprinted forward and completed four sequential back handsprings. I stuck the landing and threw my fists into the air.

"Yes!" I yelled, unable to contain my excitement.

My chest rose and fell rapidly, my lungs trying to replace the oxygen I had just used up. Blood rushed through my veins and my ears filled with a swooshing sound. My breathing was so heavy that, at first, I didn't hear the sound of clapping.

"*Magnifique!*" shouted Chloe.

She floated over to us. She wore her signature uniform of black spandex, silk scarf, and ballet slippers. Her hair was pulled into a low bun.

Coach Amy jogged over to gave me a high five.

"Nailed it!" she said, her own cheeks flushed. "That's the best I've seen you do it yet."

"*Oui*," added Chloe. "*Très bon!*"

I wiped the sweat from my eyes and smiled.

"Thanks!" I said, giving Coach Amy a hopeful look.

Maybe Chloe was finally coming around to my side after all.

"I'm glad you liked it," I continued, not wanting to waste this rare opportunity. "I thought it would be the perfect way to end the routine."

Chloe thought for a second. Her eyes darting back and forth as she replayed the moves in her head.

"Perhaps," she finally said. "I might make one teeny weeny suggestion. I think it would be more elegant if you finished with the pirouettes rather than the handsprings."

I frowned.

"But that's the fastest series of the whole pass," I explained. "It's a strong statement and a lasting impression to leave with the judges."

Chloe tapped her index finger against her mouth, unconvinced.

"What if we reworked the jumping sequence a bit?" she continued. "Like this . . ."

She placed her right leg in front of her left, toes facing one another. Then she raised one arm out to the side, the other up into the air.

"Classic croisé position to start," she began. "Beautiful, no?"

Then, she danced across the mat in a series of small, light, and airy jumps, linked together by fast, detailed footwork. She finished with a curtsy and awaited my reaction.

"But my leaps were much more impressive," I argued, heat rising from the base of my neck. "Those jumps are so tiny. They won't impress the judges as much."

"Of course they will," Chloe insisted. "They are much more beautiful. We must not forget the virtuosity of the routine."

"The what?" I asked. My frustration was about to reach a boiling point.

"Virtuosity," she repeated. "It means artistry, the degree of rhythmic harmony between the dancer and her dance."

She repeated her demonstration again as if that would help me understand. I couldn't believe it. In a matter of seconds, Chloe had managed to completely change one of the most complicated passes of my career.

From the corner of my eye, I noticed Suzanna on the far side of the room. She and Coach Mike were high-fiving and celebrating some sort of victory.

Suddenly, the reality of my situation sunk in. With two weeks until the state championship, my routine was in shambles. I had no theme, no music, no choreography, and, worst of all, no idea how to fix it.

"Louie? Are you feeling OK?" asked Coach Amy. "You don't look so hot."

The room started to spin. I had to get out of here fast.

"No," I said. I grabbed my bag and sprinted for the door. "I don't feel good at all."

When I skidded to a stop in our driveway, I noticed a pile of backpacks on the porch and a tangle of bikes on the lawn. I found Rana, Maya, and Alana inside. They sat at the kitchen table, enjoying Dad's famous pork dumplings.

"You have to try these!" Alana said when I entered the room. A trickle of soy sauce dripped from her chin.

I dropped my bag and fell into an empty chair. The warm scent of sesame oil filled the air as Dad whipped up another batch. Alana pushed the dumplings toward me, but I was too upset to eat.

"No thanks," I mumbled. I passed them on to Maya, who happily scooped up another helping. "What are you guys doing here, anyway?"

Rana wiped her mouth with a paper napkin and set down her fork.

"We came over as soon as we heard," she said. "We figured you'd be upset."

I looked at her, confused. Had they somehow witnessed my meltdown at the Gym?

"What are you talking about?" I asked.

Before she could answer, Dad walked over and placed a hand on my shoulder.

"The Spring Blossom Festival," he said sadly. "It's been canceled."

NINE

A New Idea

In my surprise, I nearly knocked the plate of dumplings off the table.

"What?" I asked, jumping to my feet. "When did this happen?"

Dad sat down in my empty chair.

"This afternoon," he explained. "Apparently, there was a waterline break at Town Park. The fields are soaked and there's no way to drain them in time. The Cape Cultural Committee has asked all around. But at such short notice, it's impossible to find another location."

He wiped his fingers on the towel tied around his belt loop. A smear of sauce stained the fabric.

"I'm sorry, Louie," he said. "We were all looking forward to your first tea ceremony. Hopefully they will reschedule it. But I don't have any more information than that."

Something sizzled on the stove and the hint of something burnt crept into the air. Dad jumped up to investigate. Once the dumplings were in the clear, he turned off the heat and placed a lid on the pan.

"Be right back," he said, noticing more stains on his button-down shirt. "I'm a mess."

I walked over to the refrigerator and poured myself a glass of milk before joining the girls at the table. As I mulled over the new information, they sat silently, awaiting my reaction. Finally, I placed my glass on the table.

"This is the best news I've heard all day!" I said.

Alana dropped her fork onto the table. The metal clanged loudly against the porcelain plate.

"Excuse me?" she asked.

I wiped the milk mustache from my lips and plucked a dumpling from the tray. The delightful flavors of fatty pork mixed with tangy scallions lit up my taste buds.

"You heard me," I said and grabbed the plate. "This is great news! Now, I can stop taking those boring tea lessons and spend my mornings training at the Gym. This couldn't have come at a better time, too. I need every bit of extra practice I can get."

Silence hung in the air as the girls exchanged worried glances.

"What?" I asked, wiping my mouth. "Why do you look so upset?"

Rana cleared her throat, as if she was considering what to say.

"Don't you think your grandmother will be upset?" she asked. "She's really been looking forward to the festival."

"Remember last week when she showed us pictures of your mom performing her first tea ceremony?" Maya added. "She was really excited."

"It's like that time my dad found his old peewee hockey jersey and wanted me to wear it under mine," said Alana. "But, you know, not as weird."

I splurged on a third dumpling and waved my hands in the air.

"Nah," I said dismissively. "She'll be fine. There's always next year. I'm sure she'll get over it."

But the second I poked my head in Halmeoni's dimly lit room, I realized I couldn't have been more wrong.

"Halmeoni?" I asked, straining to see in the fading light. "Are you in there?"

A shadowy figure sat slumped on the bed. I walked over and switched on the bedside table lamp, shocked to find her crying softly into a linen handkerchief. I wrapped my arms around her in a hug, desperately trying to make her feel better.

"I heard about the Spring Blossom Festival." I dabbed at her tear-stained cheeks. "I'm sorry."

Halmeoni smiled weakly and patted my hands.

"Forgive me," Halmeoni said. "I am acting like a child. It's just I have looked forward to the day when I could watch my granddaughter perform the *darye*. I suppose I was too overly excited."

My stomach tangled in knots. Stinging tears threatened my eyes. Seeing my grandmother this upset made me realize how careless I had been the past few weeks.

All this time, Halmeoni had been sharing a beautiful gift with me. But all I had cared about was my own agenda. My own routine.

"I suppose there's always next year." She forced a fake smile.

I wracked my brain, searching for a way to help. I jumped up, eager to busy myself.

"I can ask Coach Amy if we can use the Gym," I suggested. "I'm sure she'd let us! I am going to call her right now and get a date on the calendar."

But Halmeoni shook her head and reached for my hands. She pulled me back onto the bed.

"No, no," she said calmly, wiping away the last tears. "That is sweet of you, my love, but the Spring Blossom Festival needs to be hosted outside. It is, after all, an important time to celebrate and give thanks to nature."

I nodded glumly. Somehow, seeing how important the *darye* was to Halmeoni, made it more important to me. Suddenly, I wanted a chance to perform it. To prove to Halmeoni that I had been paying attention and that I respected our culture and its traditions.

"Besides," Halmeoni continued, "the *darye* is such a beautiful dance. It really should be held under the blossoms, the greatest stage of all. Don't you agree?"

Her words triggered something deep within my heart. Instantly, an idea took root.

"Halmeoni?" I asked. "Can you repeat that, please?"

TEN

A Cup of Tea

The most important performance of my life was less than thirty seconds away. The state championship. I sat on my knees in the center of the mat, waiting for the opening notes of music to fill the air.

The arena was packed, every row stuffed with supportive family and friends. Dancers from across the state filled the sidelines. Shiny new leotards cast a rainbow across the room.

Some girls stretched, while others paced, watching their competitors' every move. A few kept their heads down and earphones in. Most were friendly, exchanging words of support or a wave. Their coaches chatted with one another, commenting on scores and making predictions.

At this point in the day, all of the girls had completed their routines. All except me. Thanks to a lucky pick in the lottery, I had the advantage of going last and knowing exactly what needed to be done to bring home the win.

On the flip side, that meant I had spent all day watching impressive routine after impressive routine. I had used every breathing exercise in the book to keep my nerves down.

From their designated spot on the sidelines, Coach Amy and Chloe smiled anxiously. They wore matching blue jackets with the hot pink Gym logo stamped on the chest. Despite the wardrobe change, Chloe's scarf was around her neck, and her nail polish sparkled beneath the lights.

Rana, Alana, and Maya waved from the stands. Behind them, my family watched from their usual positions. Dad was on his feet, arms across his chest. Mom shielded her eyes, and Halmeoni sat up straight.

I locked eyes with her and smiled. Moments before leaving the house earlier this morning, I had pulled her aside and shared a secret.

"This routine is dedicated to you," I said. "Thank you for all that you have taught me."

I couldn't believe that I hadn't seen it sooner. The perfect theme had been staring me in the face all month long. When I ran the idea by Coach Amy, she had loved it. Surprisingly, so had Chloe.

"A tea ceremony?" she had said. "How beautiful! But it is so different than anything you've wanted so far. What about strength?"

"I realized that there are lots of ways to define strength." I shrugged. "Strong can be beautiful, and beautiful can be strong."

We had worked fast from that day forward, choreographing a routine inspired by the *darye*.

Coach Amy had checked the rule book. "As long as no actual water is used, you can use the tea set as a prop in the routine."

We had even found a seamstress who could create a costume leotard inspired by Halmeoni's *hanbok*. It was blue on top and light pink on the bottom. A strip of white at the neck represented the collar. A piece of raspberry across the chest mimicked the sash.

Planning a routine in less than two weeks was a difficult task for even the most talented team. But I was determined to make Halmeoni proud. Now, the moment of truth had finally arrived.

"Ladies and gentlemen," a faraway voice announced over the speakers. "The final performance of today's State Championship competition. Miss Louie Lin."

A hush fell over the crowd. The plucky strums of the *gayageum* filled the air. I checked in with my body, sending oxygen to each muscle and thanking them for what they were about to do.

For the first sequence, I reached forward and lifted the red linen napkin off of Halmeoni's jade tea set. Its wooden tray rested in the middle of the mat.

I moved gracefully, demonstrating the steps of the *darye* from start to finish. When it was complete, I carefully lifted the tray and carried it to a far corner, transitioning into the main part of the dance. Surprisingly, it hadn't been too tricky weaving elements of the tea ceremony into my routine.

I started with a series of three leaps, my legs long and lean, toes pointed powerfully. In between each leap, I lifted my hands to my lips, representing the ceremonial three sips. After that came a somersault sequence meant to represent the boiling water of the tea kettle.

Then, Chloe had choreographed a brilliant moment where I pretended to serve each corner of the room. My hands were placed gracefully on top of one another, protecting the invisible *hanbok* sleeves.

As the performance continued, I moved in and out of tumbling passes with ease. I moved freely and got lost in the soothing music. As I allowed myself to let go, I felt a deeper connection with the routine. I finally understood what Chloe and Halmeoni had been trying to teach me.

When the final notes drifted away, I stood silently in the center of the mat, calm and serene. It was a different departure from my usual style. But, although it wasn't my most physically challenging, it had absolutely been my strongest.

The audience rose to their feet in applause. I searched the crowd. My eyes met Halmeoni's once again. She smiled and wiped away a tear, a happy one this time.

"Way to go, Louie!" shouted Coach Amy. She tackled me in a bear hug as I exited the mat. "I'm so proud of you!"

I laughed and hugged her back as we walked to the scoring bench.

"That was very strong," whispered Chloe as she huddled next to me.

"And beautiful," I added with a wink.

Unlike my last competition, the judges wasted no time. Within minutes, they had made their decision and entered their scores into the system.

"OK," said Coach Amy, returning to competition mode. "Suzanna leads the pack with a 19.2. That will be hard to beat, but if you can manage a score of 17.5 or higher, you make the podium."

A series of bright red numbers began to flash before my eyes. One at a time, in painful slow motion, the three scores appeared.

TECHNICAL SCORE: 7.0

ARTISTIC SCORE: 9.0

"That's her highest artistic score of the season!" shouted Rana.

I turned around, not surprised to find my friends, once again, sitting directly behind me. Somehow, they had managed to make it halfway across the stadium in time to support me as the scores came in.

"Here we go," whispered Coach Amy. "Moment of truth."

EXECUTION SCORE: 4.0

FINAL SCORE: 20.0

"You won!" shouted Chloe.

"You won!" shouted Coach Amy.

But I hadn't heard either of them. The crowds cheered and my fellow dancers applauded. I sprinted toward the spot near the railing where Mom, Dad, and Halmeoni waited for me.

I jumped into the stands. I stretched my arms around my mom in a celebratory hug, toes pointed, fingers stretched. Dad cheered. Halmeoni and I smiled.

A few days later, Maya interviewed me for her *Cape Chronicle* article. She asked whether or not I had been nervous going into my final performance.

"You looked so calm and collected," she said. "Was it all just a piece of cake?"

I laughed and shook my head. A gold medal hung proudly from my neck.

"No," I answered. "It was a cup of tea."

ABOUT THE AUTHOR

Brigitte Cooper is a kid lit author, stripes enthusiast and all-around word nerd! She loves sports and once pitched under the bright lights when her Little League softball team, The Dodgers, made the championships! She lives in Greenwich, CT with her kind and funny husband, and enjoys visiting her hometown in Northeastern Pennsylvania. She is lucky to have amazing family, friends, and four furry sidekicks, including an orange kitty named Ginger.

ABOUT THE ILLUSTRATOR

Tim Heitz is an LA based illustrator from St. Louis, Missouri. He began doodling at age 3, went on to receive his Associate in Fine Arts from St. Louis Community College at Florissant Valley and then moved to California, where he finished his studies at San Jose State University, graduating with a Bachelors in Fine Arts (emphasis in animation/illustration). Tim then began his career as a Story Artist in Feature Animation and freelance illustrator for children's books.